The Dalai Lama
Peacemaker from Tibet

Chris Gibb

RAINTREE
STECK-VAUGHN
PUBLISHERS

A Harcourt Company

Austin   New York
www.raintreesteckvaughn.com

Cover: The Dalai Lama in 1996
Title page: The Dalai Lama in Mussoorie, India, in 1959

The publisher would like to thank the following for permission to reproduce their pictures:
AKG 18; Camera Press 11, 14, 16, 19t, 19b, 21, 44; Chris Gibb 20, 22, 31, 32, 34, 35, 37; Corbis (title page) 27, 29, 30, 36, 40; Eye Ubiquitous 7, 13; Hodder Wayland 17; Hulton Getty 9; Popperfoto (cover), 5, 6, 10, 12, 24, 26, 38, 39, 41, 42; Tibet Images 8, 23, 43, 45; Topham 4, 15, 18, 25, 28, 33.

Copyright Permissions, Steck-Vaughn Company,
P.O. Box 26015, Austin, TX 78755.

Published by Raintree Steck-Vaughn Publishers,
an imprint of Steck-Vaughn Company

Library of Congress Cataloging-in-Publication Data is available upon request.

ISBN 0-7398-5520-4

Printed in Italy. Bound in the United States.

1 2 3 4 5 6 7 8 9 0 LB 06 05 04 03 02

MAR - - 2008

Contents

Lhasa Erupts

As evening fell on March 9, 1959, Lhasa, the holy city of Tibet, was gripped by anger and fear. After nine years of occupation by the Chinese, the inhabitants suspected that their beloved spiritual leader, the Dalai Lama, was about to be kidnapped and taken to China as a prisoner.

Before anyone settled down to sleep that night, the people began to arm themselves with any weapons that came to hand. Nobody was going to allow the invaders to steal their Dalai Lama without a struggle.

Communist Chinese soldiers standing guard near the Tibetan border in April 1959.

Before dawn the next morning, thousands of Tibetans streamed out of Lhasa toward the Summer Palace, where the young Dalai Lama was staying. The mood of the crowd was ugly, and despite the Dalai Lama's pleas for them to go home, the people refused. Fighting soon started and before long the surrounding Chinese armies moved in with great force. The Dalai Lama made the bitter decision to escape over the mountains into India. Ten days later, many of the Tibetan people were massacred.

The Dalai Lama has never been able to return to Tibet, but his peaceful campaigning for freedom for his country, and all oppressed people, has inspired the whole world.

"One of the most important things is compassion. You cannot buy it in one of New York's big shops. You cannot produce it by machine. But by inner development—yes!"
The Dalai Lama, speaking about the importance of respecting and caring for others.

The Dalai Lama (center, on white pony) during the long journey to India.

Tibet and Buddhism

Tibet is a vast and beautiful country. Surrounded by mountains, and cut off from the outside world, the way of life of the Tibetan people remained unchanged for hundreds of years.

The Buddhist religion came to Tibet from India in about 500 A.D. Like the other major religions of the world, its main focus is on compassion. This means being sympathetic to all people's feelings and experiences. Unlike most other major religions, Buddhists also believe in "reincarnation." This is the idea that after an individual dies, his or her spirit returns to earth in another body. This may take the form of another human, an animal, or even an insect.

This map shows Tibet as it was when the Dalai Lama was born.

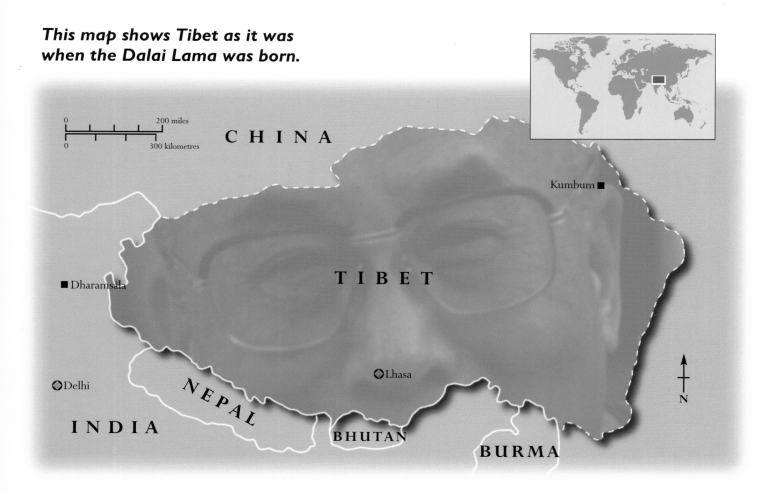

0 — 200 miles
0 — 300 kilometres

CHINA

Kumbum ■

TIBET

■ Dharamsala

◯ Delhi

NEPAL

◯ Lhasa

INDIA

BHUTAN

BURMA

N

Buddhist prayer flags flutter in front of the beautiful and isolated Yambulagang Monastery.

Tibetans soon adopted the Buddhist way of life, and monasteries and nunneries were set up throughout the country. Many had their own "reincarnated" monk or nun. The first Dalai Lama (the most honored monk in Tibetan Buddhism) was born in the 14th century. He and the following Dalai Lamas were to become the spiritual leaders of their country.

"For many Tibetans life was hard; but in the life among our mountains there was perhaps more peace than there is in most cities of the world." The Dalai Lama, writing about life in Tibet before the Chinese invasion.

Early Life

Tenzin Gyatso, the fourteenth Dalai Lama, was born in 1935 near Kumbum Monastery in eastern Tibet. His first impression of the world would have been his village—a few stone houses and a simple Buddhist shrine.

His parents were farmers who owned a few small fields of barley. They kept yaks to plow the fields. The yaks also provided meat, leather for clothes, and milk to make butter and butter tea. Butter tea was—and still is— a very important part of the Tibetan diet.

"Butter tea, mixed with salt, is the only gift a very poor people can give to a visitor— and give it they do, cup after cup."
Sir Charles Bell, a British Resident in Lhasa in the 1920s.

Takster, the area in Tibet where Tenzin Gyatso was born.

Each day began in the same way. The children threw back their yak-skin rugs and followed their mother onto the flat roof of the house. There she would light a small fire and make an offering to Buddha. All across the valley came the sweet smell of juniper and the singing of prayers.

Tenzin's family were not rich, but they lived in a community where people looked after each other. Tenzin played like any other Tibetan child—hide-and-seek, flying kites, and wrestling with his older brother. Neither he nor his brother had any idea of what lay ahead.

Tenzin's mother would have carried her children on her back, like this Tibetan mother.

The Search for the New Dalai Lama

The Tibetans believe that each new Dalai Lama is the reincarnation of the previous one. The thirteenth Dalai Lama died in 1934, and soon after important religious leaders started looking for signs and visions that might lead them to the reincarnated Dalai Lama.

Members of the search party noticed that the thirteenth Dalai Lama was looking to the northeast when he died. When they visited a sacred lake, they saw a vision of the hills of eastern Tibet. Among the hills was a huge monastery with roofs of green and gold, where a small child was playing outside a house with a light blue roof.

The thirteenth Dalai Lama, (seated, center) surrounded by his staff in traditional dress.

So a party journeyed northeast to the great monastery of Kumbum, and found a house with a light blue roof. Inside was a young child. When he saw the Abbot of Sera, the leader of the party, the child clambered onto his knee. He asked if he might have the beautiful rosary hanging around the elderly Abbot's neck. The rosary had belonged to the thirteenth Dalai Lama. When offered two identical sets of drums, beads, and walking sticks, he always chose those belonging to the previous Dalai Lama.

The members of the search party were delighted. His Holiness the Fourteenth Dalai Lama had been found.

"Even as a child ... he radiated calm, which is very nearly unheard of in a four-year-old. He sat through ceremonies which would tax even an adult." Ngakpa Chogyam, a Tibetan biographer, writing about the Dalai Lama as a young boy.

Kumbum Monastery, near the Dalai Lama's birthplace.

A Lonely Childhood

The little Dalai Lama was kept safe at Kumbum Monastery for the first year after he was found. Naturally, he missed his family and his playmates. The only companion close to his own age was his elder brother. They continued to play and wrestle together in a friendly sort of way. Sometimes they would hide for hours on end, causing widespread panic among the monks. The boys had lots of fun watching elderly lamas rush about trying to find them.

The Potala Palace in Lhasa, home of the Dalai Lamas for centuries.

An oil painting of the Dalai Lama as a young child.

> **"The young child won the immediate devotion of his people."**
> H. E. Richardson, a British resident of Lhasa during the 1930s and 1940s.

At last in 1939, just after his fourth birthday, Tenzin Gyatso began the long trip to Lhasa. The journey took many months as there were no proper roads. The new Dalai Lama was enthroned in the great Potala Palace.

Nobody who was at the ceremony could have believed that in less than twenty years the Dalai Lama and many of his people would be forced to flee their country.

Growing Up

As a boy, the Dalai Lama's favorite toy was his telescope. Perched on the high roof of the Potala Palace, he would spend hours watching the bustling life of the people below. His important religious position made it difficult for him to mix with his people, but he wanted to be one of them.

Religious studies took up much of his time. He excelled, and was soon a brilliant debater. But he was also interested in mechanical things, and here he found a friend— Heinrich Harrer.

The young Dalai Lama conducting one of his first religious ceremonies at the Johkang Temple in Lhasa.

"It was a genuine contest of wits in which the Abbot was hard put to hold his own." Heinrich Harrer, writing about the Dalai Lama's first public debate with an Abbot (religious leader) who was much older than he.

Heinrich Harrer has remained a strong supporter of the Dalai Lama and Tibet. Here, he is meeting a Tibetan in charge of refugee children in Switzerland.

Heinrich was an Austrian explorer who had spent two years crossing the Himalayas into Tibet. He became a friend of the young Dalai Lama, and taught him English and geography. Through his friendship with Heinrich, the Dalai Lama began to learn about life outside Tibet.

Heinrich also gave the Dalai Lama a lifelong interest in mechanical things. One summer, while the Dalai Lama was staying at the Summer Palace, they took apart and reassembled a motor car. It was a gift from the British, and had taken six months to cross the Himalayas. The Dalai Lama took great delight in driving it around the grounds of the palace.

Tibet and China

For centuries, an uneasy but special relationship had existed between Tibet and China. Many Chinese had been converted to Buddhism by Tibetan monks, and looked to them for help in religious matters. In return, Chinese emperors offered to support Tibet if it came under threat from other countries.

This all changed in 1910, when a Chinese warlord invaded Tibet. Revolution swept across China a year later, and the Tibetans took the opportunity to throw out all the Chinese and declare themselves independent.

Tibetan troops parade in the uniforms they wore before the Chinese invasion in 1950.

Unhappily, for the next forty years most of the world remained unaware of what was happening in Tibet. During the Dalai Lama's youth, Tibet was closed to visitors and so remained the "Forbidden Land" for all but a handful of foreigners.

Tibet had cut itself off from the world, and this was to be its downfall. The two lamas who acted as leaders during the Dalai Lama's youth did nothing to modernize the country. Noble families and some monasteries were very wealthy, while many peasants lived in poverty.

When the Communists under Mao Tse-tung won the civil war in China in 1949, Mao announced his intention of liberating Tibet from what he saw as an unequal society. He wanted to add it to the "big family of the People's Republic of China." He also believed that its natural resources—forests, minerals, and land—could be of great benefit to China.

Chairman Mao, the leader of China from 1949 until 1976. He was determined to bring Tibet under Chinese rule.

"The evil omens multiplied...and when one day in blazing summer water began to flow from the roof of the temple, the people were beside themselves with terror." Heinrich Harrer, describing how fearful Tibetans were at the idea of Chinese rule.

Invasion

In the autumn of 1950, a young British radio operator named Robert Ford spoke to the governor of one of the eastern provinces of Tibet. "The Chinese cannot hope to reach Lhasa this year," said the governor. "They will not try before the spring." The Englishman agreed with him.

A week later, on October 7, the Chinese invaded. The young radioman was to spend four years in a Chinese labor camp.

Chinese troops marching across Tibetan highlands in October 1950.

Armed Chinese soldiers guarding Tibetan fighters who have been forced to give up their guns.

The small Tibetan army had no chance. Within weeks the invaders were approaching the capital, Lhasa. The young Dalai Lama, only 15 years old, was urged by his advisors to take control. His first action was to contact the United Nations, but as Tibet was not a member, his appeal went unanswered.

Urged to escape to India, the Dalai Lama made it as far as the border before deciding to return to Lhasa. Although he knew he was taking a great risk, he preferred to face this disaster with his people.

A Chinese communist leader reads a statement to a crowd of Tibetans, ordering that the Tibetan local government cease to exist.

"As long as the people of Tibet are compelled by force to become a part of China, the present invasion will be the grossest [worst] instance of the violation of the weak by the strong."
The Dalai Lama's appeal to the United Nations in 1950.

19

Changes in Tibet

Without support from the United Nations, Tibet as an independent nation ceased to exist. The Dalai Lama had no option but to try to negotiate with the much greater force that was occupying his country. In central Tibet, the Chinese at first promised to respect the Tibetan way of life. But in eastern Tibet, they immediately began demanding money and food. They destroyed monasteries and took away people's land and cattle. Fear of famine haunted the land. Before long, the Chinese promises to respect the Tibetans' way of life were being broken throughout the country.

Nevertheless, the Dalai Lama was determined to work with the Chinese. Like them, he thought that land should be distributed more equally. However, he was very worried by their beliefs that nobody should have any private possessions and that religion should be abolished.

The Tashilumpo Monastery, south of Lhasa, was one of many destroyed by Communist Chinese troops.

"When the Chinese first came in 1950, they gave the farmers tools and said they had come to help us. But four years later, they had taken everything for themselves."
A Tibetan farmer describing the behavior of the Chinese in Tibet.

In 1954, the Dalai Lama visited Beijing, the capital of China. There he met Mao Tse-tung and other Communist leaders. Although the meeting was friendly, the two parties disagreed with one another about the future of Tibet. The Chinese wanted to rule Tibet. The Dalai Lama believed that change was necessary, but he wanted the Tibetans to be in control of change. The seriousness of the situation came home to him when he made the long journey back to Lhasa. He became aware that his whole country was like a ticking time-bomb waiting to blow up.

The Dalai Lama (second from right) and Panchen Lama (another important Buddhist monk) are welcomed by the Chinese in Beijing. The talks there were not as successful as the Tibetans had hoped they might be.

Tragedy Unfolding

The Chinese didn't understand the strong independent feeling of the Tibetans, but this isn't altogether surprising. Certainly, many Tibetans lived in poverty and life was often difficult.

Yet despite these hardships, it seems that strong traditions and a common religion united the people of Tibet. There has never been a peasant uprising in Tibet, which contrasts strongly with the many revolts that have taken place in China. The differences between the two countries led to misunderstandings that were to have terrible results for Tibetans and their country.

Although the traditional Tibetan way of life was harsh at times, most Tibetans were content to live simply. This farmer is using his yak to plow his fields.

細菌炸弹

人民防空 人民 人民防空靠人民

A Chinese billboard in Lhasa, showing Tibet as a nuclear testing ground and an area of nuclear waste disposal.

Of course, the Chinese had practical reasons for wishing to take over Tibet. They hoped to find precious minerals and make use of timber from the forests. Tibet also has an important geographical position, opposite India and facing Russia. The Chinese were at war with India twice in the 1960s, and were not on good terms with Russia. Tibet was therefore an ideal location for nuclear missile sites.

The Dalai Lama was well aware of all this. But he felt it was worth trying to achieve a meeting of minds.

> *"... what is most important is the fact that we Tibetans and our Chinese brothers and sisters have always been neighbors and must remain so. The only alternative for the future is to learn to get along and live in harmony with our neighbors."*
> The Dalai Lama, on how the relationship between Tibet and China could be improved.

Uprising and Exile

In 1956, the Dalai Lama visited India, where he received a warm welcome. On his arrival in Delhi he made a speech near the memorial to Mahatma Gandhi. Gandhi was the Indian leader who championed the idea of non-violent protest. The Dalai Lama talked about peace.

On his return to Tibet, he heard horrific stories of torture and executions by the Chinese army. Some Tibetans were fighting back, and these resistance fighters were moving closer and closer to Lhasa. The Dalai Lama realized that his country would not be at peace for some time.

The Dalai Lama (second from right), having laid a wreath on the shrine of Mahatma Gandhi in India.

> *"Non-violence is the only moral course—this is clearly in accordance with the teachings of Lord Buddha, and as the religious leader of Tibet I was bound to uphold it."*
> The Dalai Lama

Trucks transporting Chinese troops and supplies make their way toward Lhasa in 1959.

By March 1959, the resistance had arrived outside the city. Their presence was one reason for the fighting that erupted.

The rising anger of his people left the Dalai Lama in a terrible position. He was totally against violence of any kind, but found it hard to criticize his countrymen and women who were fighting in his name. He pleaded with the Chinese for peace, but to no avail. Exile was the only option left.

Escape to India

Leaving Lhasa was not easy. After praying for the last time in the serenity of his chapel, the Dalai Lama changed into the simple clothes of a common soldier. With a rifle slung over his shoulder, he and a small party slipped unnoticed out into the darkness.

The first few miles were very dangerous, for the group had to pass close by the Chinese camp. They then headed toward the wilderness of southern Tibet.

The following days were filled with endless riding through sheer valleys and across high passes—a time of discomfort, cold, and great sorrow.

During a pause in the long journey to India, the Dalai Lama (center, in dark robes) sits with his guards.

The Dalai Lama (third from left) arrives in India to a warm welcome, in April 1959.

Tibetans and supporters of the Dalai Lama waited anxiously, thinking that the Dalai Lama might have been kidnapped or killed in some remote pass of the Himalayas. When he arrived in India, exhausted but relieved, he was given a rapturous reception by the Indian people and the world's press. But the news from Tibet was grim. Many of the Dalai Lama's supporters in Lhasa had been massacred, his palace bombarded, and the Chinese were now in power.

"There is no basis whatever in history for the Chinese claim that Tibet was part of China."
The Dalai Lama

Reign of Terror

Prior to 1950, the lives of the Tibetan people had changed little over the centuries. The traditional culture remained strong, and the country was largely untouched by outside influences.

Following the brutal suppression of the uprising in Lhasa in 1959, the Chinese swiftly set about trying to destroy everything that over the centuries had made Tibet unique.

Tibetan soldiers file out of the Potala Palace to surrender to the Chinese Communists, in May 1959.

Some Tibetans managed to flee Tibet after the Chinese invasion. This woman is hoping to find safety in Nepal.

"When we saw our most venerable Lamas, who were our 'Gods' just a few days before, carrying human excrement and sprinkling it over a new-made Chinese vegetable garden, many shed tears." Dawa Norbu, author of *Red Star Over Tibet,* a book about the Chinese occupation of Tibet.

The Chinese set up government in Lhasa. All those who were thought to have helped or even sympathized with the recent uprising were in danger. Important citizens were humiliated, imprisoned, and often shot. Lamas and monks were dealt with especially harshly. Monasteries were emptied and the buildings destroyed.

Nor did the poorest peasants escape. Thousands were hauled off to work camps for supporting the Dalai Lama, or trying to hide their small stock of barley from Chinese soldiers.

Although the United Nations described the Chinese treatment of the Tibetan people as "genocide," they still took no action against the Chinese.

The Cultural Revolution

In 1966, a movement called the "Cultural Revolution" was launched in China. One of the aims was to destroy everything to do with the past. Three-quarters of China's historical monuments were destroyed at this time. Previously honored leaders were spat on and pelted with mud in the streets. Many people from the towns were forced to work in the country.

In Tibet, the Cultural Revolution led to another wave of destruction against Buddhist shrines and monasteries. Communist soldiers invaded Tibet's holiest shrine—the Johkang Temple in Lhasa—and smashed all the holy statues and images they could find. The great monastery of Ganden, near Lhasa, once the home of over 6,000 monks, was reduced to a pile of rubble. Perhaps most heartbreaking of all, 60 percent of all Tibet's sacred Buddhist literature was deliberately burned. More people were arrested and imprisoned.

Students and teachers march through Beijing during the Cultural Revolution, in support of Chairman Mao. Their banners read "Raise High Mao Tse-tung's Thoughts and Great Red Flag."

The Chinese call Tibet "the Western treasure house"—with good reason, for the country is rich in a wide variety of minerals, including uranium, oil, coal, copper, and gold. The Communists started mining as fast as they could. Forests in eastern Tibet are still being felled at the rate of one truckload a minute.

The monastery of Ganden once housed over 6,000 monks. It was totally destroyed by Chinese troops.

"The destruction was wholesale and calculated. Every building of religious or historical importance was destroyed. . . . It was an attempt at the extermination of an entire culture." Simon Normanton, from *Tibet, The Lost Civilization.*

Hope Fades

Today Chinese soldiers are a common sight on the streets of Lhasa.

The death of Mao Tse-tung in 1976 brought a glimmer of hope to Tibetans. The new Chinese leaders admitted that they had caused problems in the country. Representatives of the Dalai Lama were invited to visit Tibet. They were deeply shocked.

Everywhere they saw abandoned monasteries: of 3,500 monasteries and libraries, fewer than a hundred were left standing. Holy images had been broken and defaced.

Worse still was the Chinese treatment of Tibetan people. Even today the difference between the positions of Tibetans and Chinese in Tibet is marked. In the major towns, Chinese now outnumber Tibetans. They usually have the best housing, electricity, water, and sewers. Many Tibetans have none of these basic things.

"Nearly everyone you see is Chinese, and the odd Tibetan in the street reminded me of the Australian Aborigines—reduced to a tourist attraction in their own country."
An Australian tourist in Lhasa in the 1990s.

The brief moment of hope did not last. The Tibetan people were determined to win the right to rule themselves. They had met travelers from other countries, and heard about places in the world where people could follow their religion freely. The Chinese would not give up any of their power, and riots broke out again.

By 1987, Tibetans were again being beaten, arrested, tortured, and shot. Thousands fled their country.

Buddhist monks in the streets of Lhasa in 1987, demonstrating against continued Chinese occupation.

In Exile

While Tibetans were made prisoners in their own country, the Dalai Lama was setting up a safe haven for the Tibetan refugees in India. He made his headquarters at Dharamsala, a beautiful old British settlement that lies at the foot of the first towering rock barrier of the Himalayas. The Dalai Lama's most pressing problem was taking care of the thousands of refugees flooding across the border. Groups of Tibetan refugees still seek safety in India today.

Refugees in Dharamsala have come from all walks of life—high Lamas, nomads, nobles, peasants. Many were forced to abandon their families when they escaped. Some of the children who arrive in Dharamsala are orphans.

A view of terraced fields and the snowy Himalayas from Dharamsala.

Traditional Tibetan celebrations such as this "Lama Dance" in Dharamsala, India, help keep the Tibetan culture alive.

One of the main concerns of the Dalai Lama, and his government in exile, is that education, health care, and the celebration of Tibetan culture are continued. The majority of refugees left Tibet with nothing and now face all the difficulties of adapting to a strange culture and a different climate. The Indian government has been very generous, granting settlements and land to refugees in many parts of India.

"The Indian government still shows the greatest generosity, help, and understanding." The Dalai Lama, in 2001.

Long Years in India

The Dalai Lama has taken a personal interest in establishing the Tibetan community at Dharamsala. Schools have been set up so that, for the first time in Tibetan history, children from all walks of life now receive a full-time education.

Handicraft industries producing beautiful carpets and other traditional objects have been established, providing work for skilled Tibetan men and women. Hospitals have been built and new monasteries founded.

Children studying at the Tibetans' Children's Village in Dharamsala.

> *"The development of a kind heart [is important] for everyone regardless of race, religion, or politics. It is for anyone who thinks of himself or herself as a member of the human race."*
> The Dalai Lama

Here at least, the Tibetans can follow their religion in peace.

As long as Tibet remains occupied by the Chinese, Dharamsala continues to be the Dalai Lama's home. Here he carries on with his religious studies and teachings—these will always be his most important concerns. He has also made the system of government in exile democratic, so that everyone can vote for the government in exile. This is a major change from the traditional Tibetan system.

Ever since he was a boy, poring over his atlas with Heinrich Harrer in Lhasa, the Dalai Lama has loved the idea of travel. His exile from Tibet has given him the opportunity to travel the world over.

Tibetan monks in a procession through Dharamsala, where they can practice Buddhism without fear of violence.

37

A Universal Appeal

Despite all the suffering of his people and himself, and in some ways because of it, the Dalai Lama has become a truly international figure. He has been invited to many different countries, and people from all walks of life, races, and religions flock to hear him speak. Indeed, many of the world's political and religious leaders have spent hours talking with the Dalai Lama.

His message does not concern only the problems of Tibet, although he does feel them very deeply. Nor does he appeal only to Buddhists. Instead, he makes a plea to all people who have a sense of compassion and justice.

The Dalai Lama meeting with United States President Bill Clinton, in 2000.

His starting point is that human beings all want happiness rather than suffering. This applies as much to nations as to ordinary people. Greed and selfishness cause wars; compassion and understanding avoid and heal them.

> *"I believe in tolerance for all—so long as all have a 'good heart.'"*
> The Dalai Lama

The Dalai Lama praying at the Wailing Wall in Jerusalem, wearing a Jewish yarmulka, or skullcap. The Dalai Lama believes that people of different religions should respect one another.

World Peace

In 1984, the Dalai Lama wrote a book called *A Human Approach to World Peace*. He starts with us—you and me. How do we feel? Do we have a selfish approach to others and use them for our own gain? Or do we try to understand and help our fellow human beings? Only when we can answer "yes" to the last question can we hope to achieve peace.

> *"If we do not believe that we really are part of one human family, we cannot hope to overcome the dangers to our very existence—let alone bring about peace and happiness."*
> The Dalai Lama

Photographers from around the world take pictures of the Dalai Lama as he speaks to a crowd of monks in the Indian Himalayas. People throughout the world are moved by his message of peace.

Inner peace, calmness, and compassion are the key words of the Dalai Lama's book. He also asks for a greater understanding between different religions, nations and political systems. Much of the world has an "us and them" attitude that divides people and countries and leads to war and poverty. The Dalai Lama believes that if we discard such ideas, then we can achieve great things.

The Dalai Lama doesn't have the bitterness one might expect of an exiled leader, who has suffered the destruction of his culture and his people. This is partly what makes his words so powerful.

The Dalai Lama with Archbishop Desmond Tutu, who campaigned against apartheid in South Africa. Although the two men are of different religions, they have similar beliefs about the need for compassion in order to solve problems.

The Karmapa Lama

In Tibetan Buddhism, there are many different religious leaders. One of the most important is the Karmapa Lama.

In the year 2000, the seventeenth Karmapa Lama, age 15, made a spectacular escape to India. His journey was very similar to the Dalai Lama's in 1959. The Dalai Lama was delighted to welcome the young monk to the Tibetan community in Dharamsala.

"He has his own deep spirituality—and cheerful optimism." Trea Wiltshire, writing about the Karmapa Lama in the *Guardian* newspaper in 2001.

Ugyen Trinley Dorje, the seventeenth Karmapa Lama.

The Karmapa Lama has settled at the monastery of Gyuto, near Dharamsala. He spends most of his day in study and meditation. The monastery has become a place of pilgrimage for many Tibetans.

For many Tibetan exiles, the arrival of the Karmapa Lama brought hope. Some think that one day he will take on the mantle of the much-loved Dalai Lama, and help to focus world attention on the plight of Tibetans in exile. The Dalai Lama himself believes that the Karmapa Lama will continue to spread Buddhist ideas and teach people the importance of compassion and peace.

Gyuto Monastery, the home of the Karmapa Lama near Dharamsala.

The Laughing Buddha

"Do you think Buddhism is best?" asked somebody from the audience during a talk by the Dalai Lama in London in 1988. His Holiness laughed, and replied that the Dalai Lama was likely to think Buddhism was best—but it was only best for him, and something else could be best for somebody else. This acceptance of different ideas and religions is something that sets the Dalai Lama apart from many other religious teachers.

Some people make others laugh and smile all the time. The Dalai Lama is one of them. When asked a more difficult question about Buddhism, he cocked his head, wearing an expression that clearly said, "You don't expect me to answer that, do you?" He went on to give a talk that left the hall spellbound. He then gave a mischievous grin. "Well, that's what I think, anyway." His sense of humor and constant smile have led some of his followers to call him "the Laughing Buddha."

More than 40,000 people gather in Central Park in New York to hear the Dalai Lama speak, in August 1999.

> *"I pay tribute to our brave Chinese brothers and sisters who have also made tremendous sacrifices for freedom and democracy in China."*
>
> The Dalai Lama in 2001, talking about how many Chinese have suffered under Communist rule.

The Dalai Lama greets admirers outside a Buddhist Center in London, England.

After years of campaigning for Tibetan freedom, the Dalai Lama remains full of courage and hope. For his compassion and concern for all people, and his belief in non-violence in a violent world, he is unique. He was awarded the Nobel Peace Prize in 1989.

Glossary

Abbot The head of a monastery of monks.

Aborigines Native peoples of a country, especially Australia.

Apartheid Racial separation of people—making one more superior to others.

Buddhism The religion that grew from the first Buddha.

Campaign A series of protests and activities designed to bring about change.

Civilization A particularly advanced way of life.

Communism A belief that people should share things equally. Communist countries are often run by a police state.

Democracy A system of government where people are allowed to vote for their rules and leaders, and can express their opinions.

Dictatorship When a ruler holds total power over a country.

Exile A person who is forced to leave his or her country, perhaps forever.

Extermination When something is totally destroyed.

Genocide The deliberate destruction of an entire people.

Independent Free to govern yourself.

Labor camp A prison where people are made to work against their will.

Lama A Tibetan religious leader.

Liberate To free people from invaders.

Monasteries and Nunneries Places where monks and nuns live and pray.

Nuclear missile sites Where weapons of mass destruction are placed.

Persecute To mistreat people because of their beliefs.

Reincarnation Being born into another life after death.

Revolution An uprising against a government.

Tolerance Accepting other people's points of view.

Traditional Ways of life that have lasted a long time.

United Nations A world organization based in New York that tries to stop violence between countries and to help people.

Further Information

Books to Read:

Gibb, Christopher. *The Dalai Lama.* New York: Exeley Publications, 1990.

Pandell, Karen. *Learning from the Dalai Lama: Secrets of the Wheel of Time.* New York: Dutton, 1995.

Snelling, John. *New Perspectives: Buddhism.* Boston, MA: Element Books Ltd., 2000.

Stewart, Whitney. *A&E Biography: The 14th Dalai Lama.* Minneapolis, MN: Lerner Publishing Group, 2000.

Date Chart

500 A.D. The Buddhist religion comes to Tibet from India.

July 6, 1935 Birth of Tenzin Gyatso, the fourteenth Dalai Lama.

1937 The Dalai Lama is found by a search party from Lhasa.

February 22, 1940 The Dalai Lama is enthroned in Lhasa.

1949 The Communists win the civil war in China.

October 7, 1950 The Chinese invade Tibet.

1950 The Dalai Lama assumes full power at the age of 15. Tibet makes an appeal for help to the United Nations, but is rejected.

1953 Communist reforms are imposed on eastern Tibet.

1954 The Dalai Lama travels to Beijing and meets Communist leaders.

1956 The Dalai Lama visits India.

1956–1959 Revolts continue in eastern Tibet. Tibetan fighters move west toward Lhasa.

1959 The Tibetan Uprising in Lhasa occurs on March 10. The Dalai Lama escapes to India. The uprising is ruthlessly crushed. Full Communist reforms are imposed in Tibet. The United Nations condemns Chinese atrocities.

1960 The Dalai Lama sets up his government in exile at Dharamsala, north India.

1963 A new democratic constitution for Tibet is issued by the Dalai Lama from Dharamsala.

1966 The beginning of the Cultural Revolution in China brings much destruction in Tibet.

1967 The Dalai Lama makes his first tour to the Far East.

1973 The Dalai Lama's first visit to Britain and Europe.

1976 Mao Tse-tung, leader of Communist China, dies.

1979 The first delegation of Tibetan refugees visits Tibet.

1981 The Dalai Lama makes major tours of Great Britain and the United States.

1984 Tibet is opened up to individual tourists. The Dalai Lama writes *A Human Approach to World Peace.*

1984 Ugyen Trinley Dorje, the seventeenth Karmapa Lama, is born.

1987 The Dalai Lama suggests a peace plan to China. It is refused. Serious riots break out in Lhasa. Tibet is closed again to individual travelers—and has remained so ever since.

1989 The Dalai Lama is awarded the Nobel Peace Prize.

2000 The Karmapa Lama makes a dramatic escape to India.

2001 The Dalai Lama sends a message of peace to China.

Index

All numbers in **bold** refer to pictures as well as text.